THE CAT WHO WOULD BE KING

BETHANY HOEFLICH

To Allegra
Thank you for the inspiration!

1

THE REPORTER PAUSES OUTSIDE THE TAVERN AND DOUBLE CHECKS his itinerary.

7:30 pm Interview with Bastien I.

It's no more believable now than it was the first time he'd read the note, tucked under the corner of his typewriter. He scoffs at the name—Bastien I—the same name as the former king of Qar. Obviously, someone is trying to prank him. He's the newest hire at the printing press, and while he knows he'll have to earn his way to the top like everyone else, he hadn't expected his colleagues to stoop this low, especially when everything depends on him writing a sensational article. Something that will wow his superiors and secure his position at the press.

His last place of employment laughed him out the door after a string of mediocre pieces, but was it his fault the sleepy little town had nothing more interesting to report on than a missing pig or a raccoon massacring the pies at the annual bake-off? He's tasted the mayor's wife's huckleberry pie, and honestly, the raccoon had done them all a favor.

No doubt his coworkers have heard about the debacle and seek to destroy his reputation here as well.

Well, the joke's on them. He'll go inside, have a few drinks on the newspaper's coin, then leave with a pleasant distraction on his arm. Then he'll saunter into work tomorrow with a bounce in his step and a grin on his face. That'll show them.

And who knows? Perhaps he'll uncover a juicy story after all.

The tavern is dark, but not overly so. The wooden tables and chairs are standard, but the lacy window treatments, handwoven rug, and fresh bouquets on every table give the room a homey feel. About a dozen patrons recline about the room, sipping on drinks and dining on roast pheasant. One group sits in the back, playing a good-natured game of cards. A serving girl walks by with a tray of cherry tarts, and the reporter leans into the sweet smell as his stomach rumbles.

The barkeep slings his towel over his shoulder and leans a hairy elbow on the counter, motioning for the reporter to take a seat. Behind the counter next to a trough of ice, a long-haired orange cat rests on a silken cushion, dipping its paw in a carafe of cream before licking it off. The reporter's lip curls. That can't possibly be up to health codes. Well, he'll be sure to order a beverage that requires neither ice nor cream, lest it be garnished with fur.

Baffled, the reporter settles into a chair by the window and meticulously arranges his notepad and pencil on the table before him. It never hurts to be prepared for inspiration.

A perky brunette with a mole on her cheek and a smile that promises a steady influx of tips approaches the table. "Can I get you something, Sugar?"

The reporter returns the smile, already imagining taking

her home after the tavern closes. Perhaps this night won't be a total waste after all. He orders a pint and settles in, looking out the window. People pass by on the sidewalk, some with a purposeful clip to their stride as if they're trying to hurry home. Others stroll, arm-in-arm, enjoying the cool autumn breeze and the golden glow of the sunset.

"Excuse me, but would you happen to be Thomas Kane from The Daily Gazette?"

"Why yes, I—" The reporter swings around to greet the owner of a rich, baritone voice "—am."

There is no one there.

His ears must be playing tricks on him. He could have sworn someone had spoken to him, but no one is nearby. He slides a frown toward his pint, which he hasn't touched yet. That is his first pint, right? Yes, it has to be. His mouth still tastes of the peppermint candy he enjoyed on his way to the tavern rather than the heady flavor of fermented hops and grains.

"I do hate to bother you, but I believe we have an interview scheduled, and I'm quite desperate to get back to my nap."

No one has approached, and the only glances being thrown his way are ones of concern for his sanity. Thomas shakes his head and sticks his fingers in his ears to clear them. His breath quickens. What is wrong with him? He must be imagining things. Yes, hasn't he been working overtime this past week? Clearly the lack of sleep is catching up with him, that's all. Didn't the voice mention a nap? It's his subconscious telling him he needs to take it easy for a while, nothing more. It might be prudent to retire early to get the extra rest.

"If you've decided against the interview, just say so. There's no need to be rude."

Voices. He's hearing voices. Thomas presses his fingertips to his temples, circling them to soothe whatever madness has overcome him. Forget the newspaper—if anyone hears of this, they'll have him dragged away to the asylum. He frowns. Actually, the voice is coming from considerably lower than he imagines—from the height of a toddler, though he can't reconcile any toddler having a voice so deep. On a whim, he glances down. The cat from behind the bar is sitting on the rug, staring at him with golden eyes that flash with something like irritation. Thomas snorts. Now he's being ridiculous, imagining a cat having a human-like depth of emotion. It's nothing but a stupid animal.

Before he can call for the serving girl to close out his barely used tab, the cat opens its mouth. "Well, then. If you're going to ignore me, I suppose I'll be on my way. Good day, sir."

Thomas freezes, eyes widening as his brain ceases to function. Did it just... He sucks in a breath and unleashes a high-pitched scream. He shoots to his feet and frantically backs away, stumbling over his chair in the process. "Demon cat!"

The tavern grinds to a halt as every gaze swings his way.

"Demon Cat?" The cat rolls its eyes and jumps onto the table. "Honestly. I'd be offended if it weren't so absurd."

This couldn't be happening. Perhaps he was having a fit, or a hallucination, or a dream. Yes, that must be it. He fell asleep at his desk and now he was having a dream, albeit an incredibly vivid, disconcerting dream, but a dream, nonetheless. He pinches the inside of his wrist and mutters, "Wake up, wake up, wake up."

4

"Bastien!" The serving girl hurries over, hands on her hips as she glares down at the cat. "What did we say about scaring the patrons?"

"I beg your pardon, madam, but I was under the impression this gentleman was aware of who I am considering he's here to interview me. If I've been mistaken, then I sincerely apologize."

The serving girl swings her attention to the reporter. "This true?"

He blinks down at her. "What?"

"You have an interview?"

Thomas fumbles at his pocket and pulls out his itinerary with a shaking hand. "I have an interview with Bastien the First, not some c-c-cat."

She stabs a finger at the cat, who now watches him with an amused grin. "That's him all right. Now sit down, you're making a scene." To the cat, she asks, "Your usual, Honey?"

"That would be delightful, thank you."

"I've gone mad." It's the only explanation that makes sense.

The sky is blue.

Water is wet.

And cats most definitely do not talk.

Thomas collapses into his chair, though he leans back to put as much distance between him and the cat as he can.

The cat cocks his head to one side, then the other, as it examines him like a bug that had just crawled out from beneath the rug. "If it's any reassurance, you don't *look* mad, but I can't say for certain. Medical school was never an option for me as the universities frown on admitting students of the feline variety."

"It's not possible. *You're* not possible."

"Improbable, not impossible," the cat counters. "It could be considered semantics, but I'd like to think that many things once improbable are made possible through imagination, ingenuity, and a questionable sense of ethics. Only a year ago, the horseless carriage was nothing but the far-fetched musings of a man, a dreamer, who had been labeled deranged and unstable. I'll bet his coin purse jangles to the tune of his laughter now that everyone—well, everyone rich enough to afford one—is driving the streets. Man's greatest barrier is that which separates his dreams from becoming reality."

Thomas's mouth opens and closes. The absurdity of the situation renders him speechless, but the quote jostles his memory. "Is that Vanderwald?"

"Indeed." The cat arches a brow. "You've read him?"

"Years ago, but I much preferred the works of Brintal and Yevera."

"To your credit, no doubt." The cat dipped his chin. "Many believe Sigmus Vanderwald to be the most dangerous wizard to have ever existed, though some prop his work up as an unattainable goal for which we should all strive. Fewer yet have the wisdom to question not whether something can be done, but rather should it. But you have not come here to debate philosophy."

The serving girl returns with a saucer of cream and a plate of thinly sliced pheasant slathered in a creamy gravy. She slides it in front of the cat, giving him a scratch behind the ears before turning away. Thomas waits until she leaves before saying, "No, though now I'm not certain why I'm here at all."

"I believe you contacted me for an interview. If I'm mistaken..."

"No, no. You are correct, though I had believed it to be a joke considering you share a name with our former king." Thomas huffs a laugh and shakes his head. "I suppose that's the most believable part of the situation now."

"I wouldn't be so sure of that," the cat purrs. "Best get comfortable and pick up your pencil. I suppose, as with most stories, I should start at the beginning..."

♦♦♦♦♦

I was born in an alley behind a watchmaker's shop on a cool April night. Like all cats, we were born blind and helpless, but our mother fussed over us, filling our bellies with warm milk before we fell asleep in a comforting pile of claws and fur. The weeks went by, and while the rest of my littermates were content to sit and be groomed, I wanted none of our mother's doting. I wanted adventure. I wanted to see more than just dingy cobbles and crumbling brick.

I grew quickly. Each day, I wandered farther from her protection, confident I could handle whatever life threw at me. It became a game. How far could I go before Mother caught me and dragged me home by the scruff of my neck?

She warned me that I'd regret straying too far from home, but I, in my infinite eight-week-old wisdom, decided that she was simply determined to ruin my fun.

Before long, a sleek black tomcat moved in next door and claimed the bakery as his hunting grounds, killing as many rats as he could. The baker grew fond of him, often sneaking day-old meat pies to the rake. Fewer rats meant more hunger for us, and Mother wouldn't tolerate our pawing any longer. She took a fancy to the tomcat, and soon, my littermates and I were on our own.

That was perfectly fine with me. The docks were more to my liking anyway. Fresh fish every day? Yes, please. Fishermen were often losing bits of their haul—not enough to catch notice, but for a cat, it made the difference between a full belly and going to sleep hungry. A fish here, a prawn there. And I was more than happy to gobble them up the moment they hit the ground. It became a new sort of game, for I wasn't the only one taking advantage of the scraps. Other cats prowled the docks, so I had to be faster, smarter than them unless I wanted to resort to sneaking bites from the chum buckets.

For two years, I focused on survival and little else until the day everything changed.

The docks were bustling with activity that morning. A storm was brewing—violent from the look of the clouds that rolled in across the horizon. The fishermen trickled in with the last haul of the day before the weather forced them to take shelter. I couldn't believe my luck. Quick hands often turned careless while they rushed through the work.

Licking my lips after scarfing down a sardine that I'd managed to liberate from an unattended bait bucket, I weaved my way through the crowd and trotted past the crab stall without a second glance. I wouldn't make the mistake of swiping one of them again. I'd learned that lesson the hard way. Besides, my favorite fisherman was just ahead. He was blind and mostly deaf, and he smelled of seawater and black licorice. I could have robbed his stall without any real effort, but I wouldn't. He was a kind man who would sometimes lay out fish heads and tails for the stray cats that frequented the wharf, myself included.

But before I reached his stall, I spotted a silver plate on the cobbles, tucked away at the mouth of an alley, and on it was a prime cut of swordfish.

A more experienced, wiser cat would have been suspicious, but my mouth watered at the temptation. That fillet would sustain me for the whole day. I could slowly devour the feast then take a nap in a quiet corner without a worry until the next morning. No need to work. No need to dodge the crushing throng of haggling peasants. No need to settle for scraps.

A whole gorgeous fillet, all for me.

Hunger overruled my common sense. Before I could change my mind—or lose my meal to an opportunistic cat—I snatched the fillet off the plate and darted into the nearest alley. Eager to enjoy my meal, I crouched behind a stack of empty crates and tore into the meat. The flesh was sweet and delicious with just a touch of salt. Lovely. It was the best meal I'd had in months, maybe my whole life.

Soon, my eyes grew heavy. Nothing alarming, mind you. I normally settled in for a nap after a large meal, but I usually groomed myself first. I couldn't figure out what was amiss. Unnatural sleep pressed in, and I was unable to fight it.

The last thing I saw was a cloth sack and knobby fingers reaching for me.

I woke sometime later in a dark room that smelled of earth and mildew. My head pounded frightfully. I tried to push myself up on trembling legs, only to fall back down again. Cold metal cut into my paws. I sniffed, picking up the sharp tang of damp iron. I crept forward a few inches before banging into metal bars. A cage?

Breathing heavily, I studied my surroundings.

There were four walls and no windows. Based on the smell and coolness of the air, I judged the room to be underground somewhere, though I couldn't tell how deep. Candlelight flickered on the stone walls. Despite the poor lighting, I made out a metal table with straps fixed to the corners in the center of the room. A tray holding all sorts of sharp objects lay on the edge of the table. A small cot was shoved up against the far wall.

Voices sounded from outside the room. I tensed as they grew closer, wanting nothing more than to dart under the cot and hide until they passed. Being trapped in a cage in the open left me feeling exposed and vulnerable.

The metal door cracked open and two men entered. The first was a reedy man wearing a flat cap and threadbare trousers whose face reminded me of a rabbit. The other was tall and straight-backed with dark hair that hung in a curtain around his sharp face. Hands clasped behind his back, he crossed the room to my cage in smooth, confident strides. The stench of death and decay clung to his waistcoat like a perfume. He bent to examine me, eyes squinting as he took in every inch. His lip curled.

"Wherever did you find this one?" The tenor of his voice reminded me of a tomcat's throaty growl, making me want to press my belly to the ground and hiss.

"Over by the docks." This man wasn't nearly as terrifying. His voice was like the incessant squeaking of a neglected wheel. Or a terrified mouse. He hovered by the door, hands

10

twitching, and he couldn't seem to keep his eyes focused on a single thing. They jumped around constantly as if he expected danger in every shadow. I'd met plenty of cats like him—weak and scared. They never lasted long in this world. He wrung his hands together as if in prayer. "Lots o' strays at the docks."

"Lots of strays, you say, yet this is the one you brought me?" He didn't raise his voice, but the change in the other man was immediate. His eyes widened and his heart rate sped up.

"Well, the others are far too clever, you see." He removed his hat and ran a trembling hand through his thinning brown hair. "None would touch the bit o' fish I left out 'cept this one. He grabbed it right away, he did."

"I have no use for stupid beasts. I need one that's intelligent, cunning." He gave the man a measured look, and I got the impression he was no longer referring to cats. While the first man started to sweat, the tall one crossed the room and pulled a bottle from a cabinet, followed by a glass. He poured himself a drink, then settled into a chair, crossing his leg at the knee.

The first man twisted his hat in his hands. "Give it a chance, boss. What could it hurt?"

"Other than being a colossal waste of my time and resources? Time is running out, and I can't afford to waste another moment on faulty specimens. The experiment must be perfect."

"If I might suggest... why not use this one to get the kinks out, eh? That way you'll know you have it right for the next one."

"Hmm..." The tall man looked at me with disdain. "He's

going to die anyway. Perhaps it would be wise to run through the experiment one more time."

The first man deflated, letting out a shaky breath.

"But Evans? Don't fail me again. Bring me the perfect specimen, or don't bother coming back at all."

Evans paled and hurried out of the room. The tall man returned his focus to me. He tugged on a pair of leather gloves, then pulled some sort of metal device out of his coat pocket. My nose twitched as I struggled to make sense of what it was. He unlatched the door of my cage and swung it open, perhaps counting on the lingering sedative to keep me docile. I still might have chanced escape anyway, but the firm grip of his fist and the tick in his jaw cautioned me against defying this man. With brutal efficiency, he held the device to my ears, then eyes. He jammed his dexterous fingers into my mouth, examining my teeth and throat. Finally, he ran his hands down every inch of my body and took measurements, jotting them down on a piece of parchment. It was most undignified. I hated water, but I would have gladly doused myself in the sea to wash away the feel of his hands on my body.

And did it stop there? Oh no.

He grabbed me by the scruff of the neck, and I growled, stretching with my claws to tear him to shreds. I did not appreciate being treated like a kitten. But instead of releasing me as any sane human would, he carried me over to the table.

The straps on the table took on a new meaning. I struggled in earnest, scratching and biting and wiggling, but his grip did not relent. I had no idea what he meant to do with me, but I knew I wanted no part of it.

Soon, I was stretched out face down on the table,

completely helpless thanks to the straps fastened above each of my paws. The man uncovered a bizarre device that looked like a metal bowl with, you guessed it, more straps. He rammed that onto my head, squishing my ears in the worst way. And if that wasn't enough, he pulled a syringe out of his coat like a magician might pull a rabbit from his hat, brandishing with a flourish as though I should be impressed. The thing bit worse than fleas.

Honestly, I'd rather have the fleas.

I expected to fall asleep as I had after eating the fish, but this was far worse. Rather than rendering me unconscious, whatever he'd injected me with merely took away my ability to move. I tracked the man as he connected wires from the helmet to a metal box of some sort.

He grinned at me, teeth bared with predatory intent. "I doubt you'll survive, cat, but best of luck, nonetheless."

And with that, he flipped a switch.

2

THE CAT PAUSES HIS STORY AND STARES OFF INTO THE DISTANCE. Thomas leans forward, his tight grip nearly snapping his pencil in two. This is the story he'd been looking for, full of drama, mystery, tragedy.

"Well? What happened next?"

The cat's whiskers twitch, and he laps at the bowl of cream before answering in a measured voice, "I believe I blacked out for a few minutes, and when I woke up, he had shoved me back into the cage."

"Wait, that's it?" Thomas leans back and barks out a disbelieving laugh. "What happened? What do you remember? I want to know everything."

"It's interesting to me how those who are farthest removed demand details, expecting a victim to relive their trauma to satiate petty curiosity."

"But you must remember something," Thomas insists.

"I remember nothing," he turns the full force of his haunted eyes on the reporter, "though I suppose you'll say that's a blessing."

The full force of the lie hits Thomas, and for a moment, he

swears he can hear inhuman yowling and smell hot metal and burning fur. The reporter ducks his head, looking properly chagrined. "Of course. What happened next?"

"The cage was bare save for a dingy old grain sack I imagined was meant to pass for a blanket or cushion..."

My entire body trembled. I couldn't move without pain shooting through my skull and down my limbs. There was a time when I'd been kicked by a donkey, but the pain I'd experienced then was nothing compared to the pain I felt after this lunatic stripped me down to my most primal form before piecing me back together. I was a jigsaw puzzle that had been scrambled and reassembled, but the pieces no longer fit the right way.

My movement must have alerted the man, a wizard I decided. "Ah, I see you've survived. Congratulations." His lips twitched into the barest semblance of a smile, though his words were drier than week-old anchovies that had baked to the cobbles under the summer sun. "You're the first. It seems as though I finally got something right."

"Wh... what did you do to me?"

The wizard's mouth dropped open in shock. It took me a second to realize I'd spoken aloud. In human speak. When it finally hit me, I panicked. Cats weren't meant to speak in their barbaric tongue. I threw myself against the bars of my cage, not caring about the damage I was inflicting in my desperation to escape. The wizard crowded my cage, eyes alight with a feverish intensity that set my singed fur on edge. I pressed as far back as the bars would allow, though the minuscule distance it put between us offered only the illusion of safety.

"You can speak! This is... well, this is marvelous!" His face broke into a wide grin. Light gleaned on his teeth, sharpening his predatory looks to from menacing to down-right lethal. He raced over to his desk and knocked ink wells and letters to the floor in his haste. He returned with a clean sheet of parchment and a quill. "Tell me everything. Leave no detail out no matter how insignificant it might seem."

I stared back at him, unspeaking, my fur standing on end until I was sure I resembled a dandelion puffball. First, he tortures me, then he demands I perform like an organ grinder's monkey? Unlikely.

"Ah, forgive me. It seems we've gotten off on the wrong foot, and I would hate for that to negatively influence our working relationship moving forward. My name is Sigmus Vanderwald—"

"What?" The reporter shouts, startling everyone in a one-block radius of the tavern. He ducks his head, hiding behind his notepad as if to block the patrons' alarmed stares, and continues in a whisper, "Sigmus Vanderwald did this to you? *The* Sigmus Vanderwald!"

"Yes, him. Now stop interrupting or we'll be here all night. As I was saying..."

"My name is Sigmus Vanderwald, but you may call me Master."

Oh, he was out of his mind if he thought I would capitulate to that demand. I chose to ignore it. "You could begin by giving me some space." I wasn't a fan of feeling trapped. After being free my whole life, being shoved into a two-foot box was not working for me at all. I needed to have a clear exit. "And free me from this cage at once."

The wizard nodded as if that were to be expected. "It might be unpleasant, but your confinement is necessary at the moment. You must be restricted while you recover from the procedure, but once I'm assured of your health, we'll see about getting you settled in a more comfortable arrangement. If you behave, you might be allowed to explore the castle."

"How long?" I wasn't sure how long I could maintain my sanity at this point, though I perked up at the mention of a castle. Castle kitchens were bound to have tasty treats for me to steal, far better than the scraps I was used to getting at the docks.

"Two days at most."

Two days. It seemed like an eternity, but the hard set of his jaw warned me not to press the issue. I didn't understand what he wanted with me, so I decided to treat him like an unfamiliar tom that had wandered into my territory and test his boundaries. "That would be satisfactory. In the meantime, I will need milk, a roasted chicken leg, and someone to stroke me behind the ears."

He opened his mouth to reply, but I cut him off. "Not you. I'm not feeling particularly generous toward you at the moment."

Ten minutes later, I rested on a soft, velvet cushion,

lapping at a saucer of fresh goat's milk. A delicious piece of roasted chicken with crispy skin waited on a clay plate. I was correct. This was much nicer than anything I'd eaten at the wharf, the poisoned swordfish included. I could get used to this sort of pampering. Unfortunately, Sigmus allowed no one in his workshop, or *laboratory* as he called it, so I was bereft of ear scratches. Oh well, I suppose it could have been worse.

Sigmus removed his waistcoat and folded it on the bed, then he dragged his chair over to my cage and made a show of rolling up his sleeves to the elbows. "Now, what are you feeling? Any lingering sensations from the procedure?"

Should I answer, or would it be better to ignore him? He had delivered on almost all of my demands, so that counted for something. "I suppose there's some lethargy. A bit of a buzzing sensation in my limbs which is quite unpleasant."

And so it went on for another day and a half before I was allowed out of the cage, based on my progress. We fell into a routine. Questions, followed by a bit of freedom in the room. He did threaten to lock me back up after an unfortunate incident with his shelves of potions. I claimed no responsibility for the mess. Was it my fault he left breakable items in tall places? Hardly.

♦♦♦♦♦

"Wait a moment," the reporter interrupts. He glances down at his notes, then back up at the cat. "You broke Vanderwald's potions, allegedly valued at over one thousand gold pieces, and he didn't turn you into a cockroach or incinerate you where you stood?"

18

The cat rolls his eyes. "Firstly, I never admitted to anything. Do keep up."

"Yes, but Vanderwald was infamous for his temper. And you were the only one who—"

"*Secondly*, which is more valuable? A shelf full of trinkets, or the world's only talking cat? Make sure you write that down, and perhaps add a note about how irresponsible it is for humans to leave breakable objects where cats can reach them." He jabs a paw at the notepad.

The serving girl swings by their table while Thomas scribbles the additional notation. She winks at the cat and deftly swaps a fresh cup of coffee for the reporter's untouched pint.

After ordering a cherry tart, Thomas turns to the cat. "How did the castle staff react to you when they overheard you speaking?"

"You're assuming they ever caught on. I take great pride in the fact that the servants remained ignorant of my... abilities."

"How on earth did you manage to hide it?"

"Ahh... those were some fun days," he began.

3

THE FIRST TIME I LEFT THE LABORATORY, I FOLLOWED MY NOSE TO the kitchens. Not only would there be fresh milk and other tasty morsels, I counted on finding a surplus of rats and other vermin just waiting for me to stalk. It had been too long since I'd hunted, and I was getting antsy. You can suppress your natural instincts for only so long before you feel the madness creeping in.

The kitchen was nearly empty save for a single maid and the chef who was slumped over the table, snoring, a cleaver gripped in his hand. Admittedly, I had no idea how kitchens were meant to be run, but this seemed awfully inefficient. The poor dears must have been lacking work to keep them busy, so I decided to have some fun with them.

I stopped outside the door and called in. "You there, girl! His Lordship would like breakfast at once."

She jumped, broom in hand. "Oo's there?"

I pitched my voice higher, imitating what I remembered of Hanes's squeaky tone, throwing in just a touch of spineless panic for good measure. "Hanes. Now, prepare the food for Lord Vanderwald."

"Oo died and made 'im a lord, eh?"

Oh dear, it seems as though I'd overstepped the mark a bit. He wasn't a lord, then? Well, he had to be someone of importance to live in a castle. Then again, he did live in a dark, disgusting room... I decided to backtrack to salvage the situation. "That's not important. He requires breakfast immediately."

"But e's already 'ad breakfast."

He had?

"Are you questioning the greatest wizard who's ever lived? Should you refuse, Sigmus Vanderwald will storm down here in a fit of violent rage, transform you into a chicken, and cook you for dinner."

"Hanes? Ow'd you learn to speak fancy-like?" Her skirts swished and soft footsteps approached the doorway.

Time to make my escape.

"Prepare it, and bring it to..." I paused. Where could I say that wouldn't raise her suspicion further? I had no idea where the wizard went outside of our daily interactions. "The library."

That was a safe choice, right?

I ducked behind a tapestry before she entered the hall, hands on her hips as she glanced down the hall in both directions.

Had the chef been conscious, he might have uncovered my ruse immediately. Thankfully, the girl was so flustered she didn't bother waking him up. Instead, she hurried to fill a platter with smoked meats, fish, cheeses, bread, and butter. I licked my lips and trotted down the hall to the library to wait.

I marveled at my change in circumstance. A month ago, I'd been scrounging for scraps on the streets, dodging wagon wheels and dirty boots, wondering if each night could be my last when the battle-scarred toms came prowling. Now, I was warm and dry while I waited for the kitchen maid to deliver my meal. Not that I'd forgiven the wizard for experimenting on me against my will, mind you, but perhaps the perks were worth some discomfort.

The library was a glorious place that smelled of old books and ink. Best of all, it had east-facing windows, and I couldn't wait to claim a sunny spot for a nap after I ate. I climbed up the nearest bookshelf and curled up at the top, watching the doorway with interest.

The kitchen maid soon arrived, cradling an oversized tray in her arms. She peered suspiciously around the bookshelves. Pity she didn't think to look up.

I called down from my perch, "Very good. Leave it there on the table and begone. His Lordship wishes to dine alone and not be bothered for the remainder of the morning."

For a moment, I thought she'd drop the tray, which sent my heart into a frenzy. Sure, I'd resorted to eating worse things off the dirty cobbles before, but the idea of doing such a thing was appalling now. I was a talking cat, living in a castle, eating a breakfast worthy of a king.

I could get used to this life.

Sigmus found me hours later in a food coma. Waking me abruptly, he grabbed me by the scruff of my neck and dragged me back to the laboratory, dropping me on the table. As soon as the door was shut firmly behind him, he whirled on me. "Have you lost your senses? If you'd been discovered, all my work would have been for nothing."

"What are you going on about now?" I yawned and

stretched. "I'll have you know you interrupted a perfectly good nap."

"And that's the real tragedy, I suppose." A vein bulged in his forehead.

"Is it not?"

"You have no idea what you could have done, do you?"

"I'm reasonably certain you'll enlighten me."

The wizard paced about the room, the heels of his hands pressed to his temples. "I can't begin to impress upon you the importance of your secrecy. The servants are notorious gossips. If anyone found out about you, word would reach the king."

"Oh, would His Majesty not approve of your experimentation on poor, helpless creatures?"

"What?" His back snapped straight, and he glanced at me, confusion dancing across his face. "Oh. No, of course not. I meant that my breakthrough is not ready to be revealed."

"I don't see why not. If concern for the wellbeing of innocent animals isn't a particular hindrance of his, I'm sure he would be thrilled with your progress. Ecstatic, even."

He closed his eyes and pinched the bridge of his nose. "No. For now, this will be our secret. I'll make you a deal. If you insist on wandering about the castle, you'll do it on my orders. Think of it as a game. You are free to go anywhere you like within the castle grounds, but you'll listen to conversations and report back anything of interest you overhear."

I sat and licked a paw, not responding until Sigmus looked like he would implode on the spot. "And what do I get in return? This seems altogether one-sided."

"A plate of chicken once a day."

23

"I'm afraid I've grown bored of chicken." I took my time running my paw over my ear, licking it, and doing it again.

The wizard's eye twitched. "You will be permitted to go anywhere you please—"

"Oh, but I already *can* do that. Hardly an incentive when you're demanding I devote the majority of my time to spying. You do realize cats need fifteen hours of sleep each day, don't you?"

"You could sleep as much as you want from inside a cage."

I winced. "That won't be necessary."

"Then what do you want?" he asked, exasperated.

I crossed my paws and tilted my head, giving him my full attention. "I miss the taste of prawns from the docks, you know, before you had Hanes kidnap me." I sighed wistfully.

"Fine, a plate of prawns—"

"Fresh prawns, mind you. It wouldn't do for me to get ill from rotting seafood due to careless handling. They're freshest right off the boat, but I suppose I could compromise if they're packed in ice."

"If I'm pleased with your results, you'll earn a fresh saucer of milk each morning, and as many prawns as your furry heart desires," he said through clenched teeth.

I liked the sound of that. Still, I couldn't appear too eager. "It sounds awfully inconvenient."

Sigmus steepled his hands in front of his pinched lips and took a deep, steadying breath. "And what would you propose?"

"I'm free to roam the grounds, regardless of whether or not I happen to overhear anything, and you'll provide exactly what you promised. Plus, once per week I'll be allowed to return to my territory. Just because you managed to kidnap me and turn me into... this... doesn't mean I can neglect my home. The last thing I need is an overeager tom claiming the wharf for himself."

"Oh? And how, exactly, would you get there?" Amusement bled from his voice.

"Walking, I assume, unless you'd prefer to lend a carriage for my travels."

The wizard smiled, and I got the distinct feeling that I'd misjudged something important. He walked to the door and called over his shoulder, "Come."

My fur bristled. Was I a dog now to follow when called? Still, it wasn't like I had anything better to do at the moment. What did he want to show me? Curiosity won out and I trotted after it up the stairs, down a corridor lined with countless paintings of long-dead people, and up even more stairs. We came to the top where the path was barred by a wooden trapdoor. He shoved it open and stepped out into the sunlight, gesturing for me to join him on the battlements.

I took my time following him. There was no need to seem overeager, after all. The wizard strode over to the parapet and pointed outward. So dramatic. I jumped up on the nearest merlon and almost fell back down from shock. The height of the battlement would have been alarming enough, but the castle was surrounded by endless acres of land, forest, and homes that dotted the countryside. I couldn't smell the ocean from where we were, let alone see it, though if I squinted, I could just barely make out the roofline of the city and trails of smoke from chimneys. Walking there would take days, maybe more, and who knew what creatures lay in wait beneath the canopy of trees. If I attempted the journey alone, I would likely become something's meal before nightfall.

"What is this place?"

"This is Darnley castle, the king's country home. Of course, he isn't in residence at the moment. He and I aren't exactly on speaking terms."

"Do I dare ask why?"

"He blames me for an unfortunate incident with his favorite hunting dog, but it was hardly my fault. It's not like I intentionally made the spell go awry."

"You have a disturbing habit of experimenting on animals," I muttered.

"It's better than experimenting on humans. If an animal explodes, it's far less likely to result in my execution."

Shuddering, I took his word for it, not that I approved. As a member of the animal kingdom, it was in my better interests to oppose any sort of activities that might lead to me... exploding.

"I suppose a carriage would be the best way to travel to the city then." I refused to give up, despite the obvious wrinkle in my plan.

Sigmus weighed me with his eyes. "And what if you speak? Even accidentally. A talking cat would create a stir that's bound to reach the king."

"Please, give me some credit here. I've been an ordinary cat far longer than I've had the ability to speak in your horrible tongue. Within the city walls, I'll simply fall back on my natural instincts. You have nothing to worry about."

He didn't look reassured, though he appeared to consider my suggestion. "Perhaps a monthly, supervised visit would be acceptable. Once we're welcomed back to the king's palace in the city, you would have the freedom for a daily visit provided it doesn't interfere with your duties. Our deal would still remain, and I expect you to relay any information you overhear."

A daily visit would be ideal. I could still enjoy the comforts of living in a palace as well as the freedom to roam as I wished. Honestly, it was the best of both worlds. And if the wizard reneged on his promises of prawns and fresh milk, I could always disappear into the city, never to return. I wasn't thrilled about living on the streets in the cold and damp again; sleeping on cushions by a roaring fire had spoiled me forever for outdoor life. But now that I could speak, I was sure I could convince another family to take me in with my freakish good looks and eloquent turn of phrase. An ordinary house would pale in comparison to the luxuries I'd grown accustomed to, but it was smart to have contingencies as things rarely went according to plan.

4

THE WEEKS PASSED AND THE LEAVES BEGAN TO CHANGE COLOR and fall from the trees as the cold wind blew in from the north. Life returned to the castle as farmers sent shipments of their harvest in preparation for winter storage.

Sigmus had taken to locking himself in the laboratory for days on end, leaving me to my own devices. I should have been outraged by his neglect, but in all honesty, I needed a break. With the king still in the city, entertaining foreign dignitaries and bringing the social season to a close, my reports to the wizard had become drier than a crust of bread that had sat in the sun for the better part of the week. I'd taken to embellishing them with sordid tales of which maids were meeting the stable boy in the hay loft, which merchants were overcharging for spices, and which lady was most likely to marry this autumn. Unless something interesting happened, I'd soon start reporting on the state of the size of my bowel movements. At this point, I doubted the wizard would notice.

I began my day with a late breakfast, unaware that my world was about to change again.

The kitchens were unusually busy, but I chalked it up to winter preparations. I wasn't concerned. The kitchen maid would always spare a moment for the handsomest cat in the world—her words, not mine, though I couldn't disagree with the sentiment. She would have faced down a pack of wolves for me armed with nothing but a spatula after I'd earned her lifelong allegiance by ridding the pantry of mice, and I looked forward to my reward of daily chin rubs. The chef, however, was far less enthusiastic about my presence. He complained that I was a mangy pest and, on more than one occasion, chased me from the kitchen with a broom and a bellow that would cause battle-hardened soldiers to soil their underthings. I'd learned to time my visits for when he'd nap after the morning rush and his breathing rivaled the earth-shaking tenor of a landslide.

I was alarmed to see him still awake and red faced. I was more alarmed to see the castle stewardess, a paunchy-faced mountain of a woman who looked like she ate rocks for fun. The way her hands gripped the counter, I wouldn't have been surprised to see finger-shaped indents in the wooden butcher block.

This certainly put a damper on my plans. I had no intention of allowing that ogre of a woman to catch me lest I become intimately aware of what it felt like to be turned into a pair of fur-lined gloves.

The kitchen maid caught sight of me, and her eyes bulged. She looked away quickly so she wouldn't draw attention to me and nudged aside an empty flour sack draped over a crate. I spared a glance for the stewardess, but she was too entrenched in her conversation with the chef to notice me. I scurried over to my new hiding place and crouched behind the sack, ears twitching to eavesdrop on the conversation.

"Even if the butcher worked day and night, we wouldn't have enough in two days' time, let alone the wine. The shipment isn't scheduled for a fortnight."

"What of the larders?"

"Oh, they're filling up, but you'd better pray the king has developed a taste for boiled mush and dried beef."

"We will be prepared, no matter what it takes."

"You have some sort of magic that will turn words into food? Twenty years and he's never come this early. Why now?"

The stewardess's iron exterior crumbled leaving behind a tired shell. She sagged onto the nearest stool, shoulders hunched. "There's open rebellion in the city. The king is relocating here for his safety while the guards root out the traitors."

The chef whistled under his breath. "Aye, that'll do it I reckon."

My mind whirled with the new information. The king was coming, and in two days, no less. This was just the sort of thing the wizard would want to hear. The stewardess hovered in the kitchen for the better part of an hour while she micromanaged the patience out of the chef. With each pecking comment, his grip on the cleaver tightened and he got this maniacal gleam in his eyes, as though he was imagining chopping her up into stew. By the time she left, I truly thought she'd broken him. I thought it best to skedaddle out of there, sans chin rubs and breakfast, lest he vent his frustrations on me.

I hurried to the laboratory and meowed incessantly until

the wizard opened the door and glared down at me. His clothes were wrinkled and unwashed. Dark circles drooped beneath unfocused eyes, and his hair clung to his skull making it look thin and lifeless. He reached up to scratch his unshaven jaw and the full force of his stench walloped me in the face harder than a kick from a mule. The inside of a chamber pot would smell more pleasant.

"Ugh, you look terrible."

He slammed the door in my face.

"Oh, come now. You can hardly punish me for being honest. If you wanted a spy who showered you with unearned flattery, you should have chosen a dog rather than a cat. Now pull yourself together and let me in. I have news you'll want to hear away from prying ears. Unless, of course, you'd prefer me to wait out here and shout at you instead. I'm sure the revelation of a talking cat in the castle is exactly the sort of attention you want."

The door cracked open, and the wizard stared at me as though weighing my value against the pleasure of drowning me in a tub of water. Considering he smelled like he hadn't bathed in days, I figured I was safe from water for the time being.

"You are the singular most annoying creature I've ever had the displeasure of meeting."

"Clearly, you've never met a squirrel." I trotted inside, only to regret stepping foot into the laboratory. Piles of dirty dishes were stacked on the floor, surrounded by soiled clothes and discarded papers.

I quickly relayed the news I'd overheard, dreading having to take another breath. The wizard's face revolved through a myriad of emotions before settling on gleeful. "This is wonderful news."

"I've just told you there's open rebellion against the king and you're celebrating as though I've gifted you ten thousand sapphires and the corpse of your greatest enemy. Unless I grossly misunderstand human behavior..."

His eyes grew unfocused, and an almost dreamy countenance transformed his face from seedy degenerate to stark-raving lunatic. "What a perfect opportunity."

"So, this is a normal reaction, then?" I took a cautious step back, just in case. One could never be sure in those sorts of situations.

The wizard blinked, as if he'd forgotten I was standing there. "Hmm? Oh yes, of course. Perfectly normal and nothing to worry yourself over." He began pacing and muttering under his breath. "Must prepare. With his life threatened, it's no wonder he would retreat here to lick his wounds. It's logical. It's secluded enough from the city to deter all but the most dedicated, and the grounds are far more defensible..."

I wasn't sure what he meant, but from a cat's perspective, I had to admit that Darnley Castle was better, elevated on a sprawling hill. The surrounding land had been cleared of trees and bramble, allowing for an unobstructed view.

"And what is your plan once the king arrives?"

His smile curdled on his face and he ignored my question completely. "Continue to do what you've been instructed. Watch, listen, and stay out of my way," he snapped, escorting me out of the room with his shoe.

Outraged, I stood outside the laboratory, internally seething. How dare he? I'd been abducted, experimented on, disrespected, and conscripted into a job I hadn't even wanted, and when I finally had the first bit of decent news in weeks, he treated me like vermin. Well, if that's the sort of appreciation I could expect, he could go and find his own information.

♦♦♦♦♦

After wandering the castle for the better part of the day with nothing better to do, I'd returned to the kitchens for a snack. Now, I was regretting the decision.

"Don't know who he thinks he is," the chef muttered, punctuating his words with the steady chop of his knife through onions. "Does he think the supplies will magically resupply themselves?"

The kitchen maid crossed the room to where I waited behind a crate of turnips and *accidentally* dropped a sliver of chicken to the floor. I was more than happy to help keep the floor clean by eating it. She turned to the chef and shrugged. "Ee's the king."

The chef paused, sweat dripping down his temples, and gestured with the knife. His caterpillar eyebrows inched downward. "Have you seen his menu? Menu, pah. As if I haven't been feeding him every winter for the past twenty-five years, no complaints. My cooking has been just fine for him to stuff his gob before now."

"It can't be that bad."

"Oh, aye." The chef wiped his meaty hands on his apron and pulled a folded paper from his breast pocket. "For dinner. A whole suckling pig. Roasted turnips. Glazed carrots. Potato mash. Sprouts. Soft yeast rolls and freshly-churned butter."

"That all?"

"*That* is just one course! It goes on. We're talking haunches of venison, chicken, duck, beef tenderloins... it's obscene."

"Perhaps 'is Majesty's expecting important folk?"

"That's the kicker, isn't it? He's got no one coming the whole winter! Even told the stewardess that he wishes to overwinter by himself." He shook the paper at her. "At this rate, we'll be on starvation rations while he eats himself into unconsciousness. It's not like he can eat all this, but he'd sooner send the scraps to the pigs than to the likes of us. It's no wonder the city folk want him hanged. I have half a mind to do it myself."

The kitchen maid's face drained of color, and her eyes darted to the empty doorway. "You can't say things like that. It's treason."

"The real treason is letting common folk starve."

"You'll be swinging from the gallows if the wrong person hears."

"Let 'em hear. If they're smart, they'll agree with me." He tucked the list into his pocket and picked up the knife, venting his frustrations on the onions. "Mark my words, if it weren't for that blasted wizard lurking in the castle, the king would be welcomed with a noose instead of a feast the moment he arrived."

TWO DAYS LATER, THE CASTLE WAS IN A FLURRY OF PANIC. THE king's carriage had been spotted passing through a nearby village, and everyone was putting the finishing touches on preparations for his arrival. Sigmus flew around the laboratory with an extra spring in his step and a grin on his face. I couldn't understand his enthusiasm. From the whispers I'd heard, it sounded like he'd done something more than liquify the king's favorite dog and had been banished here to live in disgrace. Yet the chef seemed to think the wizard was protecting the king. Still, I couldn't imagine a friendly welcome, though I suppose that wasn't my business anymore.

I didn't care.

But I was curious.

I made my way up to the battlements to watch for the king. I must have drifted off at some point because shouts and the sound of a horn woke me some time later. I yawned and stretched, then jumped up on the merlon in time to see a carriage drive through the gates. A footman leaped from the back and opened the door with a flourish.

The king stepped down and paused, drinking in the sight

of the courtyard and his welcome. He wore a velvet overcoat, tan leggings, and a sable-lined cloak that looked long enough to drag in the dirt behind him as he walked. He took one step toward the receiving line and fell on his face. Gasps rang out in the courtyard.

This was the king?

If it weren't for the oversized golden crown weighed down with precious gems on his brow, I would have doubted it. He wasn't a large man, but it took an exorbitant effort to get him back on his feet. His hands shook and his face was pale. I'd seen men like this before as they stumbled out of taverns in the early morning hours, reeking of vomit and spirits.

My lips curled as I studied the king. All in all, I wasn't impressed.

Neither was the wizard, it seemed, considering I didn't spot him amongst those in the receiving line. Odd. For someone as invested in getting back in the king's good graces as he appeared to be, I would have thought he'd be the first to welcome the king to Darnley castle, bowing and debasing himself like a proper servant of the crown.

Well, it was of no consequence to me. I had thoroughly washed my paws of his schemes, and now my only desire was to see exactly what dishes were fit for a king.

I was not disappointed.

The roast duck alone was worthy of a song. Moist, tender, with the most glorious, crispy skin I'd ever tasted in a mouthful—which was all I got before the chef threatened me with a rolling pin, forcing me to flee down the hall before his aim improved.

My stomach growled. A single bite was not enough to

satisfy, and with the chef on high alert, I could hardly return to the kitchens. There was another way. Soon, the king would be sitting down to an extravagant feast. I'd just have to wait for the king to have his fill, then I could feast on the leftovers.

The thought shook me.

Settle for leftovers? Me? While I had been desperate enough to eat from rubbish bins before, I was no longer a stray. I was a talking cat—far better than a common stray—and eating leftovers was unseemly. No, I deserved the best.

Tail twitching, I detoured for the dining room.

In retrospect, it would have been better to wait, but hunger overruled common sense and propelled my paws faster.

The dining room had been transformed. What before had been an abandoned, dusty mess was now a glorious shrine to the goddess of gluttony.

My mouth watered. All that food, just for him? There was so much, I was sure he wouldn't mind sharing a bit. I crept across the room, the polished stone floor cool beneath my paws.

The servants that spotted me made frantic motions with their hands—humans were such ridiculous creatures—no doubt they wished to shower me with affection. Now was not the time. I had a mission, and it involved devouring an entire duck. Maybe two.

I jumped on a chair far enough from the king that he wouldn't feel threatened. I'd learned that lesson the hard way on the streets. It was important to give the toms a wide berth, so they knew you weren't challenging them for territory. The king didn't seem aware of my presence, so I leaned forward to nibble on some cheese that had fallen off a silver tray. A dozen soft boiled eggs rested in cups just beyond my reach. Well, those would go nicely with the cheese, wouldn't they? I just had to have one. With another glance at the king, I jumped onto the table and delicately nudged an egg with my paw. It tumbled out of its cup and rolled over to my seat. Just as I was going to crack it, I discovered the king was the rudest person in the entire kingdom.

"What's this? Shoo, I say!"

I glanced up, alarmed.

The king cried out for his guards to throw me out. Well, I wasn't about to let them get their grubby hands on me. I'd spent a solid hour grooming my coat, and I wasn't going to let them mess it up. I hopped off the table and bolted out of the dining room, not sure where I was going, only knowing that I needed to get away and hide. My paws led me back the familiar hallway that led to the laboratory. I stopped outside the door, chest heaving.

The guards' shouts had grown distant, but I couldn't risk being caught in the open. Loath as I was to accept help from the wizard after his boorish treatment, I suppose I could make an exception this once. I scratched on the door and meowed as loudly as I dared.

The moment the door cracked open, I darted inside and hopped on the desk, ignoring the wizard's spluttering protests and the ominous smell of death and decay. Perhaps I'd grown used to it during the time I'd lived in here. "What a pompous, overinflated waste of oxygen!"

The wizard froze by the door, his eyes wide and his hand frozen on the door handle. "What have you done?"

"Of course, assume this is my fault. I was merely trying to have a nice meal when the king overreacted and tried to have me thrown from the room. Would it have killed him to share a few bites?" I growled.

The wizard pinched the bridge of his nose. "He saw you?"

"Unless he has a vision impairment I'm unaware of, then I would assume he saw me."

"Don't you realize what you could have done?" he shouted. "You could have ruined everything!"

"Relax, at least he didn't hear me speak."

"You don't understand—"

"That's the trouble, isn't it? You expect me to do everything you say, but you refuse to tell me anything. You stay sequestered in here, alone, not even going to greet the king when he arrived. How are you supposed to get back in his good graces when you lurk about, hiding from everyone?"

The wizard stilled. "You think I want to get back in his good graces?"

"Why else would you do all this?"

He barked a laugh. "Oh, you poor little fool. I'm not surprised your pitiful feline brain pales in comparison to my vastly superior intellect."

A tiny kitten meow sounded from the corner of the room and I froze, my eyes bulging. The wizard's face turned from angry to sinister and his sudden smile did nothing to reassure me. Moving slowly, I crept across the floor to the cage which held three fluffy kittens. Judging by their size, they had just recently been weaned. One was black, one was tortoiseshell, and one was orange like me. Trembling, I glanced from the cage to the overlarge crate by the fire. The smell of death was stronger there, and a single black tail draped over the side. "Why... why have you done this?"

After my transformation, I'd held nothing back when he'd

asked his questions. Sigmus knew everything about how traumatizing—and painful—the process had been. He wouldn't dare repeat it. Would he?

The wizard stalked closer. "I had high hopes for you, you know. You were the first cat to survive experimentation and you could have been a glorious addition to my legacy. Unfortunately, your temperament is ill suited to working for me. I've spent countless hours poring over my calculations and notes, trying to figure out what went wrong. Do you know what I believe?"

I held my breath, not daring to even twitch a whisker.

"You're too old," he continued when I didn't answer. "Now that I have the formula perfected, I'll repeat the experiment until I succeed with a more... impressionable subject."

I chanced a glance back at the cage. The little orange kitten pressed his forehead against the bars and stretched his tiny paw as far as he could reach. "How many kittens...?"

"As many as it takes!" The wizard's eyes flashed dangerously. "Don't you understand? I've devoted my life to this. Do you think I care if a few flea-ridden pests die in the process? I would gleefully kill every cat in Qar if it meant unlocking the secrets I've chased for years."

I crouched to the floor as he drew near, pulling a syringe from the pocket of his jacket.

"And now, I have no more use for you."

"Let's not be hasty." I backed up a step. "You have no guarantee that the experiment will work a second time."

"That's a risk I'm willing to take."

Lucky for me, he'd left the door cracked open. It would only be too easy to slip past him and escape the castle. He wouldn't chase me. He'd assume I'd die within the day, and he'd probably be right. Given the choice between navigating the deadly forest or facing down a homicidal maniac, I'd take my chances with the forest. I'd just have to leave the kittens to their fate. There was nothing I could do for them.

Another meow, more pitiful than the first, made me pause as the wizard approached. There was no guarantee that the experiment would work and every probability that they would join their littermates in the crate awaiting cremation or burial. Even if it did work, and all three were given the ability to speak, what sort of future did they have here with this monster?

Back at the wharf, it was every cat for himself. If those same kittens and I had squabbled over a half-eaten fish on the docks, I would have walloped them and taken it for myself without a shred of guilt.

Could I walk out that door, leaving them in the hands of a crazed wizard?

Another meow, and I shuddered.

No, I couldn't just leave them. But what could I do?

I'd hesitated too long. The wizard was on me, one hand reaching for the scruff of my neck, the other swinging the syringe toward my side. I just barely moved in time to avoid being impaled. I spun around to face him. The needle glinted in the candlelight. He hollered as I scratched his hand. Blood pooled in four deep lines, and the syringe clattered to the floor.

He drew back his foot, no doubt to kick me, but I didn't wait for the blow to land. I snatched up the syringe in my mouth, whirling away before he could grab me. With my target gone, his momentum carried him the full way around, throwing off his balance. He crashed into the table. I couldn't help but huff a laugh as my panic melted away. This was no different than when I'd had to dodge the vicious toms that prowled the docks. *Well, perhaps a little different*, I thought as he pushed himself upright on ungainly hairless limbs. The wizard was larger, clumsier, and far stupider.

I darted beneath the cot and backed up until I hit the cool stone wall.

"I grow tired of this, cat. Give up now, and I'll make your death painless." He footsteps neared until I could see his shoes. A drop of blood splattered on the floor. "Well, mostly painless. I owe you for my hand."

I couldn't help the kittens if I was dead, and so I waited.

"You've gone mute, is that it? Pathetic creature. It's a wonder your mind wasn't crushed beneath my power."

A growl built in my throat, but I stifled it before it could escape.

"The destination is inevitable, cat, but you get to choose the road we take. If I must drag you out, I promise you will suffer."

Patience. I was the hunter, and he was my prey.

The wizard sighed. "Very well. You asked for this."

He lowered himself to his knees, hand groping blindly in the darkness beneath the cot.

I seized my chance.

Syringe clamped between my teeth, I climbed his arm as if it were a curtain. As expected, he shouted and threw himself backward to put some distance between us, but I didn't let go. I climbed higher and higher until I latched onto his face, digging my claws in deep. If he wanted to remove me, I'd be taking a chunk of him with me.

Sigmus bellowed.

Eyes closed, he pummeled me with his fists, desperately trying to knock me off, but I took each blow with newfound determination. No matter what he tried, I wouldn't budge. I wrapped my paws around his neck and, using my teeth, rammed the syringe into the base of his neck. His back arched and he tripped, falling backward into the wall. I had to hope it was enough.

I sheathed my claws and fell softly to the floor. The wizard reached a shaking hand behind his head and yanked the syringe out.

Then he laughed.

My ears flattened. I'd hoped whatever was in that syringe would be enough to at least disable the wizard if not kill him outright. Perhaps it was, but I hadn't been able to administer it properly. And now, he was laughing with murder in his eyes. My legs trembled—with fear or exhaustion, I couldn't tell the difference. In a moment, he'd have me, and there would be no saving the kittens from their horrible fate. I'd failed them. The thought hurt more than I could have imagined.

"I think I'll skin you first. You'd make a lovely pair of slippers, really. Or maybe I'll turn you into a..." His gaze unfocused and he shook his head "...a rag and use you to scrub my chamber pot."

The wizard took a step toward me and wobbled.

"Useless, wretched c-creature."

His legs gave out, and he collapsed with the force of a waterspout tearing through the bay. His hand twitched once, and then he stilled.

I didn't dare hope the wizard was dead. I wasn't that

lucky. And if I didn't get help before he woke up, we'd all be doomed.

With one last look at the kittens, I scrambled around him and out the door, heading to the one place in the castle I hadn't explored yet—the king's chambers.

6

THE DOOR WAS OPEN WHEN I SKIDDED AROUND THE CORNER, narrowly avoiding smashing into an antique urn. The guards didn't spare me a second glance as I hurried inside and immediately ground to a halt.

Was I in the right room?

I'd expected the king's chambers to be bedecked in the finest furniture and fabrics so he could bask in his riches after a long day of lording over the peasants. Instead, the room was suited more for a servant than royalty, stripped of all valuables and filled with the barest of necessities—a small wooden desk and chair, a straw-filled cot and thin wool blanket, and a cedar chest that appeared to be empty save for a single change of plain clothes.

The king himself was slumped over the desk, hands trembling as he held a quill. Wearing a white undershirt and loose cotton pants, he looked far less intimidating than he had at dinner. Deep creases marred his forehead, drawing his brows down over his eyes.

I crept forward, unsure how to approach him. An hour

ago, the king had ordered his guards to seize me for daring to eat at his table, so I gathered he wasn't a cat person. Oh well, even kings weren't perfect. As much as I wanted to blurt out my request for help, I didn't imagine he would react well to a talking cat. Whatever I did, it couldn't be rushed. I reassured myself that the wizard would take a while to wake up and recover from his injuries before resuming his experiments. I had time.

I hoped.

The quill scratched across the parchment as the king continued to write, oblivious to my presence. Well, I'd just have to warm him up to me first, then he would be sure to do as I asked. I purred and rubbed against his leg.

The king jerked in his seat. "What's this?" He squinted at me. "Well now, aren't you the same fellow from dinner?"

I meowed in response, hoping he wouldn't throw me out immediately. If he called for the guards, well, I'd have to take my chances and speak, no matter the consequences.

"I suppose I should apologize for that, shouldn't I? In my defense, I haven't been myself lately, and you were stealing my eggs."

I jumped onto his desk to get a closer look at what he was working on. It appeared to be some sort of list with scratches though the words, the penmanship growing more frantic toward the bottom of the page. I glanced back at the king. He was watching me with sad eyes, none of the ire I'd seen lingered in them. He reached out tentatively and pet me on the head. I leaned into his touch, encouraging him to get right behind the ears. Maybe he was a cat person after all. I had just resolved to plead my case when a loud knock sounded on the door.

"Come in, Rothwell."

The king's advisor, a spindly fellow whose appearance reminded me of a sapling in the midst of a hurricane, entered the room. He shuffled the stack of papers in his arms and gave a deep bow. "Sire, the remainder of your feast has been disposed of beyond the castle gates."

The king nodded and continued to stroke me behind the ears.

Rothwell stepped closer, his fingers tightening on the papers. "If I may be so bold..."

"When has that ever stopped you before?"

"Very good, sire. Wouldn't it be easier to deliver the food to the village with the compliments of the king than to keep up this ruse?"

"To what purpose? If they knew I'd given it with my blessing, they would sooner burn it than eat it. At least now when they curse my name and shake their fists to my rule, it will be with full bellies and children who will live another day."

Rothwell paused and stared at the floor as if running a myriad of responses through his mind and finding fault with them all. In a weary voice that spoke of countless lost debates he said, "It's not too late to sway their opinions of you."

"We both know that's proverbially untrue. Even if it weren't, I've earned every ounce of their hatred. I sent good men to die. Fathers, sons, brothers, sacrificed for a war I knew we could not win. I taxed them into a poverty they will never escape. No, it's better this way."

They lapsed into an uncomfortable silence.

"What of the valuables I tasked you with collecting?" the king finally asked. I took the opportunity to turn and the king pet down the length of my neck and back, causing my hindquarters to lift with each blessed stroke.

The advisor gave a little cough. "Ah, yes. I had the servants strip everything of value from the castle and deliver it to the throne room, though I can hardly imagine why. I believe the words 'dragon's hoard' and 'obscene display of wealth' were bandied about by servants who've stopped bothering to whisper their treasonous thoughts and now shout them through the halls."

The king smiled, though his eyes were filled with a deep sadness I couldn't begin to understand. "Gather everything and place it in the royal carriage. Charge a single driver to head east without guards."

"Unguarded..." The advisor's face leeched of color. "It will be set upon within a mile!"

"I sincerely hope so. I've heard rumors of a vigilante from Shirewood who revels in relieving the wealthy of their valuables and redistributing them to the impoverished masses. An unguarded royal carriage should prove an irresistible target." His chin dipped toward his chest and he took a deep breath. "I know I can't bring home their loved ones, but perhaps in this, I might begin on my path toward redemption."

"I admire your dedication, but this is an ungodly sum of money. I would have to pull together an itemized list, but judging by what I've seen, you could keep the military supplied for a decade with the wealth in the throne room alone."

"Yet compared to the worth of a life, it is not enough."

"But—"

"I'll hear no more of it."

"Very good, sire," Rothwell dipped his head in submission.

For the first time, the king turned to look at him. "Is there anything else?"

The advisor hesitated a moment, then he nodded as if to convince himself. "There is the delicate matter of your succession."

The king stiffened. "Have you located any distant relatives with a blood claim?"

"Our search has proven fruitless, I'm afraid. It's imperative that you name an heir."

"The doctor says I still have a few weeks left." Then he said quietly, as if he were trying to convince himself, "There's still time."

"In the interim, perhaps you might consider Lord Samiryl."

"Lord Samiryl is a money-hungry vulture who would sell his mother if it gained him power. I wouldn't trust him to run a bath, let alone run a country."

The advisor sighed. "I can't say I disagree with your assessment, but he is perhaps the most qualified to rule, and with few choices at your disposal it wouldn't be prudent to dismiss the idea entirely."

"Then he can pry my crown from my lifeless corpse. I'll not be responsible for unleashing him on the masses so he can treat my people like cattle. Things would have been different if Erik had survived, but that is no excuse to surrender to a transfer of power that will send Qar into the darkest age since we were overrun by the Harlnese. No," his hands tightened on my shoulders, "I will do this my way or not at all. It will be my final attempt at redeeming my countless mistakes rather than making another for the sake of ease."

"There is no shame in naming a placeholder, even one you might view as distasteful, if it means holding the kingdom together."

"I would rather name a dog as my successor than him," the king scoffed. His expression turned thoughtful. "Actually..."

He eyed me as he pulled out a fresh sheet of parchment and dipped his quill in the pot of ink. "Rothwell, what would you name this cat?"

"I beg your pardon?"

"This cat. He requires a name as regal as he is."

"Oh, well then. I suppose Bastien would do."

"Bastien," the king turned it over on his tongue as if relishing the flavor. "Yes. That will do. Bastien the First."

"If I might inquire, why are you concerned with this now?"

"Because, Rothwell, I'm declaring him to be my successor." The king held up a hand to quiet his advisor's sputtering protests. "You're right. Without the terms of succession laid out, Qar is at risk of an all-out civil war as my nobles resort to squabbling like children over something as silly as a crown. Barring the chance that a distant relative resurfaces to stake their claim, Bastien here will fill the void." The king chuckled to himself as he rolled up the scroll and sealed it with his crest. "It is done. I can't wait to see the looks on their faces when it's announced."

I was flattered, but I could wait no longer. By now, Sigmus could have awakened and snapped the kittens' necks out of spite. Still, I should acknowledge the honor the king has given me. It was only polite, after all. I sat tall and proud, curling my tail around my paws. "If that's an official job offer, I accept the position, Your Majesty."

The king's smile froze on his face and his eyes bulged. He shot out of his seat and retreated until his back hit the wall as a strangled gurgle escaped his throat. Rothwell's jaw would need surgery to reattach. The king clutched his chest and fell to his knees, one hand braced against the bearskin rug. He tried to wheeze something to Rothwell, but in an instant, his eyes rolled back into his head and he collapsed to the floor.

"Well, that was a bit of an overreaction," I said, and Rothwell ran screaming from the room.

"Wait, you caused King Rupert's death?" Thomas interrupts.

"Caused is such a strong word," the cat says. "And who's to say? He'd been in such poor health the doctors themselves marveled that he'd lasted so long. Anything could have been the catalyst, really."

"The reports said he died suddenly of a heart attack."

"Yes, well, life is such a fragile, uncertain thing." The cat lays on the table and crosses one paw over the other. "It's a stroke of luck the king was able to secure the line of succession before his untimely passing, enabling me to order Sigmus's arrest and rescue the kittens. I took them to live with me in the summer palace, and all three grew fat and pampered by the kitchen staff."

"That can't be it." Thomas shakes his head. "It doesn't seem right that Vanderwald got off so easy."

"I beg your pardon?"

Thomas's ears reddened. "A lifetime in the dungeon isn't enough for a man like him. After what he did to those kittens? He should have been made to suffer for his crimes."

"Who says he didn't?" the cat purred.

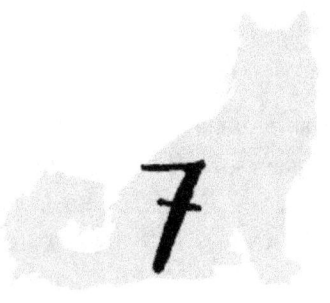

7

I SAT ON THE PLUSH THRONE, A MINIATURE GOLDEN CROWN ON the cushion next to me. I'd been all too eager to have it until Rothwell informed me it had been designed for infants. The man himself waited beside the throne; his hands folded before him. My newly devoted advisor was resplendent in a velvet doublet and buckled shoes that were flashy enough to distract the casual observer from his vapid expression which I knew masked his frustration. After the shock of losing the king had worn off, Rothwell had been all too eager to depart immediately for the capital. I staunchly refused. Once he realized I wouldn't be swayed, his face cleared of all emotion until it was as bland as a slice of toast.

He would recover from the disappointment eventually, but there was one thing I had to do first.

The doors screeched open and two guards marched inside, dragging a filthy, delirious wizard between them. His head lolled to the side and chains rattled against the floor. Compared to the arrogant, put together wizard I'd first met, Sigmus was downright feral. Stringy hair stuck out at all angles and dried blood caked to his face and hands. The guards deposited him unceremoniously before me and retreated a step, keeping their hands on the hilts of their swords.

The moment he had space the wizard launched to his feet as if he'd only been pretending to be incapacitated. He snapped his teeth at the guards, then spit on the floor before turning to face the throne. He froze when he spotted me. "You!"

Rothwell tensed, but I relaxed back on my haunches.

"Where is the king?" the wizard demanded. He spun in a circle, lips curling in a sneer. "He's too good for me now, is it? I won't forget this disrespect."

"Oh dear, it appears that no one has informed you. Pity. Do clear this up for our guest, Rothwell." I waved my paw in a regal manner.

My advisor cleared his throat. "You are honored to be in the presence of Bastien, first of his name, king of Qar, bane of rodents—"

"Don't forget devourer of crustaceans. That's my favorite part."

"—devourer of crustaceans, and defender of justice. Kneel before your king."

The wizard stared at Rothwell a long moment, perhaps waiting for the court jester to pop out of the ceiling and declare it all a cruel joke. "You mock me."

I ran a claw across the crown at my side. "While I'll admit it's difficult to take you seriously when you're in chains, no one here would dare mock you."

"Then release me and we'll finish what we started in the laboratory." He threw his shoulders back and tipped his chin up as though my obedience was a foregone conclusion.

My tail swished. "Oh, I think not."

"You're afraid."

"I'd prefer the term *reasonably cautious* but use whatever vocabulary you wish. It makes no difference to me."

"You want revenge for what I did to you. Fine. Let's get this over with."

"Are you so eager to die?" I prodded, cocking my head. I had no delusions that he was prepared for that outcome and would counter it with some sort of scientific hoo-hah I had no hope of understanding, but it did come as somewhat of a surprise that he'd gotten to the point so quickly.

Unflinching, he held my gaze. "I'm not afraid of death."

I chuckled under my breath. "Oh, my dear, ignorant wizard. You will not die today."

"I... won't?"

Was that hope lilting in his voice? It brought me a great deal of satisfaction to be able to crush it.

"You shouldn't," I amended, "but there's no guarantee when it comes to scientific experimentation, after all."

His brows furrowed.

"Confused? You shouldn't be. After all, you were kind enough to leave a copious amount of research in your laboratory, and so detailed! I've been informed that my predecessor employed a wizard who's led a revolution in the magical arts in the capital. Using your notes, he will be able to do something that has never been done before—transform a human into something entirely different. Something once believed impossible, but you and I both know the flexibility of that term by now. Isn't that marvelous?"

The wizard's face turned whiter than a fish bone. "No."

I leaned forward. "Oh, yes. Provided everything goes

accordingly, you'll be in possession of four paws and a tail in less than a fortnight, my friend. I do hope you enjoy living out the remainder of your life as a cat on the docks."

For the first time, genuine fear sparked in his eyes. "Please, give me a clean death. Anything but this."

Was I taking this too far? One thought of those three kittens and the countless others he'd already murdered, and any sympathy I might have had for him vanished.

"Take him away."

"So that's it then." Thomas rubs his forehead, a small smile on his face. "Poetic justice."

"You don't think I was too harsh?"

"Oh, no. Of course not. Some might wonder if you were too lenient with him. What's to stop the criminals if you aren't harsh with their sentences?"

"I'll never know. I kept my paws out of the criminal justice system after Sigmus. It was just as well. Rothwell kept my true identity a secret, so I settled into my role as more of a mysterious figurehead, relying on a small council to handle the daily tasks and decisions so I could be free for more important business, like a daily nap in the gardens. I attended meetings when it suited me, though the small council had no idea I was their king. To them, I was the beloved pet of their eccentric king. It was awfully tedious, and I would have skipped the meetings altogether if it hadn't been for Lady Cheryl feeding me bits of cheese under the table."

"It sounds like you had a grand time playing king, but

what of the news of your untimely demise? The papers covered your funeral."

"I can't deny I enjoyed being pampered, but I was ill-suited for the responsibility of running a kingdom. I was born for a bed by the fire, not a crown. I made the decision to quietly abdicate, naming Lady Cheryl as my successor before the elusive King Bastien the First had a tragic encounter with a boiled chicken bone."

"You named her your successor because she fed you cheese," Thomas squints, "didn't you?"

"It's as good a reason as any, wouldn't you agree?"

He shakes his head. He leans back in his chair and drops the pencil on the notepad. "And then you retired and moved here?"

"Oh, I had a few adventures along the way. There was the time I joined a pirate crew and searched for the lost treasure of Atlantis. And the time I single-handedly dissuaded the Harlnese from invading the capital. Oh, and who could forget when I rode a Singali lizard across the desert to escape a band of raiders?" Thomas gapes at him as he chuckles. "But there comes a time when something beckons you home. It stirs in your blood and calls like a siren, and nothing will quiet it except to return."

The bartender calls for final orders before closing. Thomas stares at his notes. How had the time gone by so quickly? "You've given me the framework for a sensational article. How can I ever thank you?"

"Your thanks might be a bit premature."

"What?"

"Best of luck with your article, Thomas Kane." The cat

hops off the table and stretches, kneading his paws on the rug. "Tis a pity that everyone will read it as fiction."

"What... what do you mean?"

The cat glances back over his shoulder with a rueful grin.

"Who would possibly believe a story about the cat who would be king?"

ABOUT THE AUTHOR

Bethany Hoeflich is the author of the Dreg Trilogy. She lives in Central Pennsylvania with her husband, three children and an assortment of furry (and scaly) creatures.

Monday through Friday, Bethany is at the mercy of the sadistic whims of her scatterbrained muse, feverishly churning out the words for her next novel.

On the weekends, Bethany wrestles narwhals, participates in competitive taco-eating competitions and visits alternate dimensions through a rift in her stereotypically dark and spooky basement.

www.bethanyhoeflich.com